SEXY REVENGE

Table of contents

Copyright
Dedication
Acknowledgement
Prologue
Chapter one: Leeds millionaire
Chapter two: Explosive
Chapter three: Coma
Chapter four: Ghost
Chapter five: Frank said
Chapter six: Just die
Chapter seven: Lights flash
Chapter eight: Cold then warm
Chapter nine: Stolen
Chapter ten: Physical scars
Chapter eleven: Slow dancing
Chapter twelve: Papers found
Chapter thirteen: Eviction
Chapter fourteen: Unborn
Chapter fifteen: Stolen phone
Chapter sixteen: Sophia

Chapter seventeen: Private investigator

Follow and message Anita Kirk any questions that you may have on Twitter, good reads, Linkedin and Facebook.

Written by Anita Kirk.

Dedication

This book is dedicated to Anita Kirk's husband that is always there supporting her one hundred percent with her writing journey, her mum has written two children's books herself, Jenny's Swing and Jenny's Waltz and her two lovely children that are always their to listen to her ideas and tell her what they think in a positive and impressive way.

This book is also dedicated to Anita's father that has sadly got dementia and Alzheimer's in his care home, if he knew what she had produced using her talents he would be her number one fan reading every book that she writes as he was a keen passionate reader before he became very poorly sadly forgetting everything and everyone that was his world, and that was familiar in his life.

Acknowledgments

I would like to thank you for taking your time to pick this book out from the millions of books available out there to read, if you do enjoy reading this book your review would mean the world to the author for her to enjoy reading, and sharing this book with other's on social media or in person would be most appreciated. Thank you.

Prologue

There are plenty of comical moments in this story and also there is a small amount of adult erotica content inside.
Jenson and Ella are about to get married with them being together for a year. Jenson owns plenty of property and cars with his jealous friend Frank having his beady eyes on what he owns ready to pounce in prime position when his life is about to fall to pieces with explosive very funny situations turning out to be reality.
Margo start's off a dangerous unpredictable situation with a major accident/explosion happening for Jenson to have an out-of-body experience with him feeling like a painless cloud above his body, with him watching and listening to life unfold below him for nearly four years with him unable to give his opinions with deaf ears from the living.

People get spooked and freaked out with lights, the radio and other out of the ordinary things happening because his best friend Frank steals his life hoping for him to die.

Frank is disappointed as Jenson skip's the morgue by the skin of his teeth then the cold finally wakes him up from his coma with Jenson trying to get his life back that had been stolen by Frank.

Jenson finally finds out that he has got a daughter called Violet that he had never met with him wanting to be part of the family business and have a happy ending getting married to Ella, with him finding out that she is heavily pregnant with Franks baby Sophia.

Jenson goes on a long mission to get his life back in a sneaky but clever way.

Frank goes crazy with fireworks because he knows that he is on the losing battle against Jenson and Ella.

How does Jenson get his own back?

Pubs and places in this book are real that you can visit in person.

Sexy revenge

Chapter one

Leeds millionaire

Jenson and Ella invite their close single friend Frank for a garden party with the party in full swing with everyone enjoying the music at the side of the swimming pool.

Frank speaks with a low tone, "I really would love your life Jenson and Ella instead of having my life with me not having two pennies to scratch my arse with."

Jenson replies, "If you work hard enough like me you can have my life and be a millionaire like myself, I will lend you a bit of money if you need it!"

Frank replied, "You have done well in life to get where you are, I will try my best like you have and yes that would be great and I will please lend some money off you soon because I am brassic skint like I said!"

Jenson replied, "I was speaking to my rich friend the other day, I asked him how he became a millionaire, he replied with I was a billionaire before I met my wife, and she started spending my money on anything and everything in her sight."

Frank and Ella shook their head laughing with them enjoying a few more hours outside drinking some fresh home made lemonade full of citrus lemon pieces with Frank leaving after a lovely evening.

Jenson and Ella were in the bedroom with Jenson speaking, "I can't wait for us to get married in a few weeks, I am so glad that we met last year at the alchemist food bar in Leeds, it was the best thing that I have ever done in my life meeting you, you deserve to share my millions with me, I love your body it feels so soft to touch, your soft blond long hair is amazingly perfect and your face glows with happiness when we are together and your smiley face is amazingly warm and as soft as satin!"

Ella replied, "I love your fit muscular body as well from all of your weight training, when you touch near to my clit it makes me feel electrically alive with it making me feel so excitedly turned on!"

Jenson replied, "I love tickling and touching your silky soft skin, you are my special and the one and only sun, moon and my sparkling twinkling stars!"

Ella replied, "I'm not a religious person, but I am sure that god made you for me, you have got the perfect petite bottom with a medium build, I love kissing you, your lips are always amazingly warm, tender, delicate, soft and smooth!"

Jenson's phone rang with their employee Margo on the caller identification, "I have got a really bad headache, so I am really sorry, but I am unable to work today because it is making me feel a little bit sick!"

Jenson replied, "Okay don't worry Margo, you have a rest and get yourself better me and Ella will sort it out, don't worry you will still get your full pay for it."

They put the phone down.

Ella expressed her opinion, "That means that one of us or both of us will have to step in to do Margo's work it is a good job that we only drank lemonade earlier!"

Jenson replied, "Yes, I will go, I love the wind flowing through my short black hair with the top off in our Ferrari and our Lamborghini and it feels amazing when everybody is turning their heads towards us, it makes me feel like the Queen, we can carry this on later with scented candles and a glass or three of gin to savour the mood with our low romantic naturally lightly lit gentle lighting, if I were a snowflake I would fall for you every day of my life, your hair is so soft and aromatically gorgeous and it always smells so sweet!"

Ella replied, "Okay, you are so loveable as well I was really enjoying that, what a let down with it bursting my bubble of romance and excitement, I know that you have got to go so please make sure that you drive safely, I will have a rest while you go if that is okay, you can run your fingers through my hair before you go to make it feel like a virtual hair blow, instead of the wind blowing through my hair in the car, it is much nicer when you play with it!"

Jenson replied, "Me too, you have a rest, I will get dressed now, I love you so much, and your amazing long blond hair is so pristine, it will make our sex more erotic later when I get back home to you, before I go I was reading in the newspaper that a lonely man wanted a wife within a week he had loads of replies with people saying you can have mine!"

Ella replied, "That is funny, give me a cuddle and a kiss before you go, you are so lovely."

Ella and Jenson got dressed, Jenson drove to Margo's workplace cleaning job.

Chapter two

Explosive

Jenson spoke as he got back in the car after he had finished cleaning, "I live with Ella, she is my amazingly gorgeous fiancé that I am lucky to have, I am driving back to her, my best friend Frank lives not far from us in Leeds, Yorkshire, United Kingdom, if I could choose one person to trust with our lives he would be our number one person every time.

Jenson's phone rang with Ella on the caller identification speaking, "Hi Jenson could you please get some milk on your way home!"

Jenson replied, "Of course I will yes, I will only be a few hours, and I am so happy that our cleaning business is doing very well making us lots of money from organising and cleaning peoples home interiors and shops all over the world!"

Ella replied, "Me too, I can't believe how it has taken off making our company so popular with us having a good reputation with so many excellent reviews from our customers, I love the review that says that our team are that jolly that they would invite us on holiday with them, I will let you go so that you can concentrate and drive safer on the motorway."

Jenson replied, "Yes we have got too many nice reviews to choose from and it is good when our customers want us to go on holiday with them, this obviously means that we make the most popular best team about, Okay I will go in a minute, before I go I was speaking to a man the other day, he said that he used to be a banker, but he lost interest, so he gave up!"

Ella replied, "You are funny, I always wondered why aliens hadn't visited our planet, someone said that it had got only one star, so they didn't bother."

Jenson replied, "Very funny and I hope that they do keep away because I don't want them taking you away my darling, okay bye for now take care my sweetie pie Ella, you remind me of a Christmas cracker full of love hearts that are bursting to pounce onto me full of love and passion!"

They were about to put the phone down when a waggon drove into the back of Jenson's red Ferrari, the waggon was hardly touched without a scratch with the driver walking up to Jenson apologising, "I am so sorry mate but my tyre blew out and I ended up piling into the back of you!"

Ella was shouting down the phone, "What was that loud screeching and grinding noise with another loud crashing sound that was even louder a second ago?"

Jenson's Ferrari was crushed into bits with him trapped inside and hurt badly with him muttering, "I am in so much pain what the hell was that, it is a good job that it is on hands free my phone Ella."

Ella replied, "Are you okay?"

Jenson cried, "No it is my pride and joy this car and it is ruined the same as me with this man apologising to me, I know that it was an accident but I don't know what to do with myself, all I can explain is that I almost feel paralysed!"

The petroleum wagon driver was holding his head in his hands sat on the floor at the side of Jenson's car looking very upset, "What have I done, I need a cigarette to calm my nerves?"

He lit his cigarette with petroleum leaking from Jenson's car with a man shouting from a distance, "You need to put your cigarette out before there is a fire or even worse an explosion that will cause catastrophic chaos disrupting all of our lives!"

Ella randomly shouted, "I will meet you at the hospital Jenson, Yes please put your fag out now, you are making me panic, I really do wish I was there with you, I will not be able to get to you because the road will be closed, I will set off now!"

Onlookers from other cars that had been forced to stop just looked at Jenson strange from a distance speaking loudly, "What a waste that car looks like it was expensive, I am sure that if he needs treatment I am positive that he will end up in a private hospital, I hope that his car goes up for sale because I want it!"

Jenson's phone dropped out of his hand onto the floor, "I am sorry Ella but I have just dropped my phone on to the floor of our car and nobody is getting their mitts on my pride and joy, I really wish that my head didn't hurt so much with me banging it on the seat."

The phone suddenly went dead with the car being damaged from hitting the floor and being useless because it was dead as a door nail, "That's my communication gone with Ella."

As the waggon driver put his cigarette out, "I will drive a short distance away to avoid an eruption of fire!"

There was a large boom with the petroleum waggon exploding putting Jenson and other road users in a dangerous life threatening situation.

The people that had watched the accident on the closed-circuit television above immediately dispatched ambulances, police and fire engines to Jenson with them arriving and shutting the motorway in minutes, the fire crew released Jenson from the car talking to him constantly to keep him awake, "Please don't fall asleep because we need you to stay awake with us!"

Chapter three

Coma

A lady screamed, "We are all going to be dead with the smoke, and I have just noticed that the fire is getting a lot bigger, in my opinion it will be out of control before we know it!"

Jenson muttered, "Why is it so hot and why am I in so much crippling pain in my chest from where the seatbelt is on holding me into my seat and why do I feel funny in my head and why can I not feel my legs?"

A fire fighter lady replied, "That is a lot of why's, I know that it is easy for me to say but don't worry I have just undone your seatbelt, and we will have you out of the car away from the fire any time we are cutting you out now, we can see by your face that you are in pain, I am just letting you know that a man rang the emergency services the other day with him saying that his wife had an insect bite on her clit, so they stopped having sex, I said bummer mate, he replied with oh what a good idea, he then put the phone down."

Jenson replied, "That has cheered me up a little bit, you are noisy with your tools and the vibrations are making the pain worse and I really appreciate you getting me out thank you, but I have got a request could you grab my phone from the floor so that I can ring my Ella if I can make it work!"

The fire fighter lady replied, "I can not reach into the car because your phone is buried in the car floor with the dashboard covering it and there is far too much sharp debris for me to cut myself on and it looks like your car is about to explode, but we are always here in the hour of need, two police officers crashed the other day, on the bright side I think that is the fastest response that I have ever seen without them having to phone for help."

Jenson wiped a tear away replying, "You are a joker, I am hating being in so much pain, you are making me cry with laughter for a second, but I am glad to be out of my car, I don't know if it will be able to be mended or not, can you please reach my phone now?"

An ambulance lady replied, "Don't worry about your car and your phone the police will sort it out, we are giving you morphine for the pain through your cannula that we have put into your arm, we will gently put you in the back of the ambulance now to avoid you being in more pain, you will be okay!"

A police man managed to reach Jenson's phone, "I think that I have just got the phone in time."

Another loud boom came from the waggon with a lady shouting, "It is a good job that I left my car because my precious gap insurance has come in because my car is on fire as well now, this is a majorly dangerous situation that we are in, and this heat is over powering, it is making me feel proper sweaty."

Jenson started gasping for air and wheezing while grabbing his chest and pulling a face turning hot and clammy with him making noises, groan, ouch.

"Oh no this is our worst case scenario, it looks like Jenson has gone into an unconscious cardiac arrest or into a comatose we need to resuscitate him, then put him on to this ventilator right now and get him to hospital as soon as we can before it is too late for him!"

Jenson spoke back to the ambulance lady, "Can you please tell me why I am looking down at my body with it looking very pale like I am dead from above with it looking like my spirit and some of my blood has just left with my breath, and why have you put ventilators in my mouth to keep me alive and how am I even talking and seeing myself below this is strange watching you trying to keep me alive in an outside of body feeling, I must be a ghost with you ventilating me and giving me drugs and other things that I need to stay alive and well?"

There was no answer from the ambulance crew.

Jenson spoke, "I think that I must be cracking up because I feel no pain now at least while I am just watching from above!"

The ambulance lady spoke, "We need to get his heart going again because it has stopped can you please shock him right now with the defibrillator!"

Jenson spoke, "I am here alive looking down at you working on my body please just look up at me, this is making me feel confused with my unresponsive limp body below, I feel light as a feather with what it looks like faint cloud fingers."

The other ambulance lady replied to her medical female colleague, "I think that we have got him back with us for now but for how long I don't know, I just thought that I would share with you that I tried playing hide-and-seek at the hospital the other day, but they always kept finding me in ICU?"

Chapter four

Ghost

The other ambulance lady replied, "You are daft, the other day someone asked me what a ghost would buy in a pub, he replied with boos, now that we are at the hospital lets get him inside and get going to our next victim that needs our help!"

Her colleague laughed, "I could do with some booze right now!"

Jenson was wheeled inside of the hospital and sent for X-rays and examined at his bed, then he was immediately taken down to the operating theatre for surgery on his legs.

Jenson looked down on himself from above the whole time speaking, "Why am I not waking up, as I speak I can see my mouth move slightly with nothing coming out of it with the tube in my mouth, how can I only hear myself with nobody else hearing me, I really can't be a ghost that behaves like a cloud?"

Jenson then got wheeled into his own private hospital side room after finally arriving thereafter his leg surgery was completed.

Jenson's brother Lucas was sat waiting for him, "Don't worry we will not give up on you Jenson, please come back to us, I will make sure that your Ferrari is mended for when you are better or a new one is waiting for you, a wise man told me to keep on dreaming that is why I keep on sleeping, I just hope that you are having sweet dreams!"

A police lady walked in to Jenson's room, "I have just brought Jenson's phone back that we have found in the car, I will leave it in the cupboard with the rest of his sparse belongings, I just hope that he eventually comes around again, and I am just informing you that the wagon driver has been locked up for his crime!"

Lucas replied, "Thank you for letting me know what is going on, your kind words and taking time out of your busy day fetching Jenson's phone back for him."

The police lady replied, "Your welcome, I have to go bye."

Jenson spoke, "I will come around because I need to get married, look after my cleaning business, Ella and drive my car's again, and I am here above you."

Lucas carried on with a tear in his eye, "Please come back to us we are all thinking of you, Ella told me about what has happened the police must have rung her and all the rest of the family."

Ella walked into the room, "Jenson I feel so sad that you are laying in that bed looking like you are dead, all of the rest of our family are in New York, I will keep them updated on your progress!"

Jenson replied, "If I could make myself cry to communicate with you I would."

Lucas left the hospital, "Sorry but I have got to go Jenson, you get better and come around, bye for now."

Ella waved goodbye to Lucas, "Bye Lucas we will speak again soon, I will stay a little bit longer then I have got to go myself."

Ella left kissing Jenson before leaving crying, "Frank has been very helpful to me giving me comfort already, he was immediately asking if we need any help with our business or anything when I rang him to tell him about you."

Ella eventually left weeping on her way out.

Frank arrived at the side of Jenson's bed, "Now that you are unconscious and out of my way I will be able to work hard and concentrate on enjoying your life in your shoes to the fullest that I can and enjoy your fiancée Ella in your bedroom hopefully wink wink!"

Jenson looked down replying trying to make his cloud fingers move, "You will not have anything because I will be back to myself again soon to kick your ass, you can't call me a friend any more after saying that!"

Frank did not respond or reply looking through Jenson's coat pockets, "Wow I feel like I have won the jackpot I have found your front door keys to your holiday home in New York, you always talked about how lush it is, I am looking forward to swimming in all three large pools, and driving your three large expensive cars and living in your mansion with six bedrooms and even better I have found your keys for your Leeds home where Ella lives with six bedrooms as well, so I can hopefully make her fall in love with me instead of you!"

Jenson shouted back to Frank, "You leave my beautiful Ella alone."

Chapter five

Frank said

Frank spoke, "I am really sorry Jenson, but I am definitely going to see your Ella, if anything happens between us I apologise in advance for my unacceptable sexual behaviour, but if you ever wake up I am sure that your clothes will be out of fashion the way that I feel, but someone has got to keep her company in your empty side of the bed."

Jenson spoke, "I am getting fed up with deaf ears, and when I get my hands near your neck you have had it, if only I could make other parts of my body apart from just my lips move slightly it would be a major achievement!"

Frank spoke, "I will be back again at some point, I will come with Ella next time bye for now!"

Jenson got more annoyed helplessly watching down on his body, "Come on body I am begging you please wake up and start breathing for yourself instead of having to rely on the breathing tubes and the pump!"

The doctor spoke, "I don't know when you will wake up Jenson, it could be tomorrow or it might be years from now."

Jenson asked the hospital team, "What are you doing to me now just please make me breathe."

There was no reply like he was not there with weeks passing by with him having no visitors.

Ella walked in to the room, "I am sorry that I haven't been for a while to see you Jenson, I have been to our holiday home in New York with Frank, he will be here as well in a minute, I do love you and I will always love you, but Frank said that you most probably will never wake up, I admit that I have slept with Frank because he was trying to comfort me because I was crying over you, and yes I do feel a little bit ashamed at what I have done, but just face it you are not around to give me enjoyment in the bedroom, so I had it handed on a plate to me so, I just gladly received it!"

Jenson growled with anger, "How dare you sleep with Frank, I will keep this hospital bed warm for Frank for when I get out of it!"

Frank walked in and stood at the side of Ella, "Hi, I know that you are unconscious so you will not realise that we haven't been for a few weeks, don't worry because I have been looking after Ella for you in all areas of life keeping her maintained, I will tell you a joke anyway, where do eggs go on vacation?"

Ella replied, "I wish that it was you that was answering Jenson, what is the answer, where do eggs go and yes Frank has been looking after me, I think that you should come with us when you eventually wake up, this is making me feel a little bit tearful seeing you unconscious!"

Frank kissed Ella on the cheek answering, "New Yolk city."

Ella replied, "Thank you for making me feel better again Frank you are always there to cheer me up when I am down."

Jenson felt angry replying back, "Of course I will come with you I own half of everything, you don't look like you are missing me one bit the way that you are behaving!"

They stayed a few hours then left.

Jenson spoke, "It looks like I am unconscious, but am I because I feel like I am awake?"

The nurse walked in, "I will put the radio on for you Jenson so that you have got a bit of background noise, but sadly I know that you will probably have no clue that it is on!"

Jenson was looking down at himself below with tubes and wires coming from his body, "I feel like I am a fly on the ceiling listening to music over all of the noise from the machines and watching people visit me and all I can do is watch them cry and talk over me, when I try to talk back to people all I can do is hope that people will hear me."

Jenson's brother Lucas arrived at the side of Jenson, "I have paid for you to be looked after in hospital until you finally wake up, wow that is strange how the radio stations keep randomly changing on their own, and switching between many different stations, I was listening to the orchestra on the radio earlier but there was too much sax and violin, so I turned it off."

Jenson replied, "I like that and yes that is me changing the radio stations, I wish that people could hear me."

Three years went by with Jenson watching day by day down on his body below him.

Chapter six

Just die

Every Christmas, birthday, marriage, and baby been born he watched from above feeling helpless as people celebrated around his body singing, dancing, reading, blowing bubbles and pampering him from head to foot talking to him like he was awake.

Jenson listened to Frank, "I have decided that you will not wake up, so I have been living your life enjoying running your business with Ella, thanks to you I and not poor now, I am glad that I am not living in my dingy one bedroom council flat struggling to pay my bills, the best and kindest thing for you and me to do is die so that I can enjoy your family life until I die!"

Jenson shouted back, "I am determined to wake up and get better to get my life back from you, you are a proper life wrecker!"

Frank spoke, "I am sorry but I have stolen your perfect life, and I have told your family, friends and work colleagues that you will not wake up!"

Jenson was furious hearing this news with nothing that he could do feeling very angry, "If I could just make the lights flicker on and off in this room Frank may get the message that I can hear him!"

A nurse walked in speaking to Frank, "I don't know how the lights flickered just in Jenson's room it feels very spooky and strangely odd in here like the spirit's are trying to communicate with us, I will ring the maintenance man for them to be looked at, I remember that time when the radio stations kept changing randomly a few years ago that was very bizarre too."

Jenson realised, "I just made the lights flicker with my anger towards Frank that is a start after being in this coma for three years unable to communicate, my anger must be helping my cloud fingers to touch things for real or my angry vibrations are finally doing what they needed to do."

Jenson listened to Frank, "I am dealing with my dodgy solicitors, and I am forging your signature, I apologise for signing everything over to myself that you owned, is it you making the lights flicker Jenson?"

Jenson tried to reply, "I am not surprised that I am making the lights flicker with what you are saying."

Frank spoke, "It is a little bit creepy me sat watching the lights flicker it is making me feel uncomfortable and like I want to leave."

The nurse walked in with the maintenance man, "There is nothing wrong with the lights but I will change the bulbs anyway, while I am here I have got a joke for you why did the melon enter in to the lake?"

Frank replied to the maintenance man, "Why did the melon enter in to the lake, and that is really strange with us having no power cut and the lights are in fully working order!"

The maintenance man replied, "Maybe Jenson is trying to tell you something, I don't know why these scissors are left on the worktop, I am going now because I am in demand and the answer is because they wanted to be a water melon, sorry but I have got to go now bye!"

Frank replied, "Thank you bye."

The maintenance man replied walking off, "Your welcome, no problem."

Frank whispered, "Maybe it almost feels like he is listening to me trying to communicate with me, I am really sorry but I can't apologise enough because I will try to damage your tubes to put you out of your misery sooner rather than later with these scissors, you won't be in pain anyway, the only problem is that I have got to think of an excuse what has happened to your tubes!"

Jenson yelled, "Don't you dare damage my tubes because I am looking forward to getting my own back on you and putting you in the same position as I am in."

The nurse walked in, "Don't put the scissors near to his tubes because that is what is keeping him alive, you need to watch what you are doing."

Frank replied, "I was just trying to stab a fly with it, do you know where wasps go on holiday?"

The nurse replied, "Whatever you say, I am not sure if I believe you, I nearly had to phone the police and where do wasps go on holiday?"

Frank replied, "They go to stings a pores."

Jenson replied, "The last laugh will be on you I can guarantee that, because I will definitely get my own back on you one day Frank I promise you that and it will not be a pretty outcome!"

Chapter seven

Lights flash

Frank walked out with the nurse looking at him strange asking, "Are you okay."

Frank replied , "Yes the lights just freaked me out a little bit."

Frank walked off.

Two weeks later.

Frank walked in to Jenson's room, "Your business will belong to me in the coming days, I hope that you don't wake up until the business has transferred over to me completely."

Frank walked off again.

Two weeks later Frank arrived again and sat at the side of Jenson, "I am sorry for stealing your business, but thank you for helping me change my life it is one hundred percent better, you certainly are not getting any benefits from it now with you knocking on death's door!"

Jenson got really angry again, "I remember when I slapped my violin in anger and got done for domestic violins abuse, I might get done again for domestic violence towards you."

The lights started to flash on and off again with Frank speaking, "Sorry mate but my stolen lifestyle is amazing, if you ever wake up you will be a cabbage with no recognition of your old lavish lifestyle and expensive carefree behaviour, so I think that I have done the right thing steeling your amazing high life so that me and Ella can make the most of it."

Frank mentioned to the nurse, "The lights have gone on and off again you may need the maintenance man!"

The nurse rang for the maintenance man, "He is on his way."

The same maintenance man looked at the light, "It must be just when you are here because I have checked the electric's and there is nothing wrong with the light!"

Frank got up and left in a rush muttering, "The lights in this hospital get odder!"

Lucas visited Jenson, "I have been coming to see you most days, and I have been writing down that there has been no movement from you, I hope that you will wake up soon, Frank is correct sadly I don't think that you are going to wake up!"

The nurse spoke, "I think that you have tried to keep Jenson alive on life breathing support long enough, I think that we should let him rest in piece!"

Jenson replied, "Body you really do need to show that you can wake up now."

Lucas replied, "Okay I don't want to admit it, but I think that you are right."

Jenson begged his body again, "Please wake up!"

It was his last chance to wake up.

The doctor removed his breathing tube with him still not breathing for himself.

Lucas spoke, "I think that it will be a good idea if we could try again in a few days to see if he can breathe for himself!"

Three days later they tried again to remove the tube with him breathing with no help with Lucas stood at the side of him.

Lucas screeched, "It looks like Jenson is gasping for his breath!"

The doctor replied, "I am so sorry but Jenson has stopped breathing again, I am removing all of his tubes and wires to make him look more normal!"

Jenson shouted, "I must be shallow breathing so that you can't pick it up that is all I can think of!"

The nurse replied wiping tears from her eyes, "Please say goodbye Lucas, then the porter's will take Jenson to the morgue, could you organise his funeral Lucas, I am so sorry for your loss!"

Lucas wiped his tears away replying, "Yes I will get a funeral director to organise all of my requirements, thank you for all of your help."

Jenson shouted, "I am not watching my own funeral, I suppose it will all end when they do my post-mortem, it is even sadder because I can't even make my body cry to match my emotions!"

The porters arrived, "We will take him down now!"

Jenson shouted "You need to leave me here in this warm and comfy bed and please do not put me in a cold fridge, I will definitely shiver to death then!"

A porter spoke while wheeling his covered body on the trolley, "Another person has gone from this world, and he is never to come back to this life how sad, I wonder what he was like when he was alive!"

The other porter replied, "I wonder if he was fun or boring when he was living his life?"

Jenson replied, "I am alive and I really don't like the look of it in here and I wish that you would uncover my face because I feel like I can't breathe, and I am fed up with being discussed with me unable to answer."

Chapter eight

Cold then warm

The morgue staff took over, "We will put him in the mortuary fridge, then we can do his post-mortem later on today."

Jenson replied, "What, please don't do that, I just need to move my arms at least to show that I am alive, I feel frightened for my life and claustrophobic in here."

Hours ticked by.

The post-mortem staff member spoke, "Let's get Jenson out of his cold box!"

The other staff member replied, "Look he is shaking and his fingers are moving, he must be alive, but his eyes are shut but moving with plenty of rapid dancing eye movement like they are about to open!"

Jenson suddenly woke up screaming with joy, "Finally you can all hear me, the cold must have woken me up, thank you body for not letting me be burned or berried."

The morgue staff member jumped and gasped picking the phone up shaking like a leaf with a gobsmacked look phoning the ward screaming, "You will not believe this but Jenson is alive, can you move anything else Jenson?"

Jenson replied, "No, but I feel freezing and amazed to be alive if I stand in that corner it looks to be about ninety degrees so please wheel me over there, and how long have I been unconscious?"

The morgue staff member replied, "You have got a sense of humour that is good, it will be going on four years you have been unconscious, you should warm up soon with a blanket over you and you will be on your way back to the warm ward at any minute!"

Jenson gasped, "Wow that is a long time that I was out of it!"

The porter arrived, "It is nice to meet you alive this time, have you ever kissed a person next to you when you woke up because I did, and I am not allowed on American Airlines again!"

Jenson replied, "That is funny, and it is nice to meet you again instead of above you, do you know why six was afraid of seven, and all I can say is at least I am on my way back up to a warm area where Lucas will be waiting for me, I am so glad that my mouth hasn't seized up!"

The porter replied, "That must have been strange for you waking up in a morgue, here we are you will be in your warm bed when you have been transferred over bye for now and why was six afraid of seven!"

Jenson replied, "Thank you for wheeling me back, bye mate and because seven ate nine."

The porter laughed walking away, "Oh I get it, very funny."

Everyone on the ward welcomed Jenson back with open arms including the patients.

The nurse sister in charge spoke, "I am happy that you finally came back alive."

Jenson replied, "Me too."

Lucas was ecstatic that he had woken up, "You are behaving like you have not been in a coma!"

Jenson replied, "I have watched everything that has happened, please look through my coat to see if my keys are there because I can't walk yet, I need to build my muscles back up again?"

Lucas replied, "No your keys are not in your coat pocket!"

Jenson replied, "I knew that I was seeing correct from above, I can't wait to get out of bed, Frank has got trouble coming to him!"

Lucas looked at Jenson strange, "I don't know what you are talking about you must have been dreaming because your eyes were shut the whole time when you were unconscious, but as soon as you are able to go home you can come and live with me, I have hardly seen Ella and Frank since your accident about four years ago, I tried to contact her about your finances, but she didn't want to know!"

Jenson replied, "I have got a good idea why!"

Lucas left.

A year went by with him walking short distances daily building his strength to be discharged with the discharge day arriving, "I can finally walk unaided again thank the lord."

Frank poked his head around the door, "Hi mate, we are glad to see that you are awake."

Jenson replied, "You will be pleased to see me because I have got a surprise in store for you both when I am feeling up to it."

Frank got up and left speaking, "Bye mate I have to go to Ella, I secretly think that it was you that messed with the lights above you when you were in a coma."

Jenson replied, "Yes it was me I am not joking, it is you that I will be messing around with next but not in a nice way!"

Frank just looked at Jenson, "Okay I am going because you are threatening me, all I have done is help you out making sure that Ella didn't meet someone else!"

Jenson gritted his teeth, "If that's what you call looking after Ella having her in my bed you have got a really odd point of view because she has got a new man and it is you isn't it?"

Frank stood up fast in an abrupt way and left not answering.

A week passed by.

Chapter nine

Stolen

Jenson left hospital with Lucas, "Please drive me to my house in Alwoodley, Leeds because I have not seen Ella in person to hold her in my arms in our house for nearly four years and, I am desperate to see her, I have missed her so much!"

They walked up to the gate expecting Ella to open the gate with her speaking through the tannoy on the gate, "Sorry but you don't own anything and I live with Frank now so you can't come in!"

Jenson struggled to keep calm replying, "Okay, that was a cold as ice reply with it now feeling very unusually frosty even though it physically isn't, I am glad that my Ferrari is mended and safe on the driveway, I really don't have the energy to fight with you at the moment!"

Lucas was still sat in the car outside watching the commotion happening speaking to himself, "That's disgusting behaviour for god's sake just let him in have you got no compassion you cold-blooded heartless bitch."

Jenson got back in to Lucas's car. "I need your help to get everything back because everything that I noticed when I was in a comatose is unfortunately totally unbelievably true!"

Lucas replied, "I don't know what you mean, but yes I will help you all the way after what I have just seen!"

Jenson replied, "Frank has stolen my whole life and Ella!"

Lucas replied, "You need to get everything back, I will definitely help you all the way no problem at all even if it means me getting a bit fierce and unpredictably dodgy."

Jenson replied, "Thank you for your support, I will break in and steal my keys back in the middle of the night!"

Lucas replied, "I thought that you were going to say that you will break his legs or something similar with the amount of hatred and anger that you must have towards him!"

Jenson went to live in Outwood, Wakefield with Lucas noticing that he had got his driving licence back through the post, "That is what I want to do in time to come eventually break him and at least I have got a bit of my life back finally!"

Hours later.

Jenson borrowed Lucas's phone and car and drove to his Leeds house noticing an open downstairs window with him climbing through it with him noticing that Frank was asleep on the couch with his arms tightly around Ella.

Jenson tip toed over to his keys on the table putting them in to his pocket noticing a girls shoes on the black kitchen door mat.

Jenson whispered to himself, "That is why Ella would not let me in, I will start my phone recording just in case I need precious evidence!"

A young girl walked in to the kitchen screaming, "You are my dad aren't you please tell me that I am correct?"

Jenson replied looking very surprised with his jaw lowering, "I don't know if I am it is a major surprise to me!"

The girl replied, "My name is Violet, look this is a photo of you and mum about four years ago before she knew that I would be born when I was just a butterfly in her tummy, and yes mum said that you were in a coma and Frank is my new second dad that does everything for me!"

Ella walked in heavily pregnant with a tear in her eye, "You need to go Jenson, you can obviously see with your own eyes that I have got a new life now, and I am really sorry but it doesn't involve you!"

Jenson replied, "I only found out that I have got a daughter because I broke into my own house, I find that is disgusting that you did not tell me!"

Frank walked in to the kitchen, "Sorry mate but we couldn't tell you because we thought that you were going to die and on the down side for you everything legally belongs to me and Ella now and you own nothing, you may be able to see Violet occasionally when she has got some spare time away from her usual activities that she has got to do!"

Jenson replied with an elevated angry tone, "So you have stolen my Ella, my daughter Violet, my money, my houses, my car's, is there anything left for you to take from me, do you want my blood as well?"

Frank replied, "I am really sorry Jenson that it has worked out this way, but you will have to live like I used to be forced to live, skint and lonely with no hope in the world with just your blood to keep you going."

Violet interrupted, "Frank is a good dad to me, maybe I could have double the Christmas and birthday presents this year that would be great, and extra holidays away, this is sounding very positive to me."

Jenson replied, "Yes you are a lucky girl, I can see that you are excited to see me, I have not had the chance to be a dad to you because I have been in a coma and I didn't know that you existed until now because Ella never introduced you to me even when I was unconscious, but I will try my best to make up for the lost time!"

Ella replied, "I am sorry but I think that you had better go because you are upsetting Violet."

Jenson replied, "More like upsetting you, I will go, but I know that you have used a dodgy solicitor because I heard every word that you said when I was unconscious, so I will get everything back!"

Frank replied, "You can't prove that because you have got no evidence so good luck with that and I thought that you were going to die so that is why I stole everything that you owned for us to have a good life instead of it going to Lucas and the rest of your family because they didn't need it as much as me because they are already well off."

Jenson replied, "You just admitted that you have stolen everything to me, I will leave now and make it my mission to get my own back on you, I would love to get to know you Violet!"

Chapter ten

Physical scars

Violet replied, "I am okay with my dad Frank, but yes it would be nice to get to know you!"

Jenson replied walking over to the car that Lucas had also got into while Jenson was inside, "Bye for now, I will be in touch, I am in a slight brain fog with what has happened to me, so I cannot concentrate on things for a long time, I am glad that Frank admitted on my secret phone recording that he has stolen my life."

Lucas replied, "Jump in to my car, and we will go back to my house, your legs look like they are full of scar's from your accident, I feel sad for you!"

They drove to Lucas's house with Jenson speaking, "At least I have healed now from my visible scars anyway."

Lucas replied, "Yes that is good."

Jenson replied, "My physical scars are still alive and kicking, I am going to set Frank up by making it look like he has done a bank robbery, I just need a gun to set him up with!"

Lucas replied, "How are you going to do that, I really think that I would like to be a cake robber because it would take the cake, I am just thinking I have got a gun in the loft that was left behind by the people that used to live here you can use that?"

Jenson replied, "Me too, I love cake too much as well, I will ask Frank to meet me at the bank to set up a bank account for Violet so when I get some money again I can put some into her savings account, before we go inside I will plant a gun in his bag visible to the staff so that he is contained and locked up to get rid of him so that I can steal my life back, and you are a lifesaver having a gun ready for me to use thank you!"

Lucas replied, "Your welcome, whatever you want to do I will support you!"

They drove back to Lucas's house with Jenson's ex staff member called Margo stood outside as they arrived speaking in an upset tone of voice, "I have just found out that you are here, Frank has stolen your business did you know?"

Jenson explained, "Yes I know, do you have any more proof that I can use to help me to get my life back?"

Margo cried, "I feel so sorry and sad for you, you were a good boss, I can understand why he did it because it has brought him some money that he didn't have, I only found out because I know your Leeds next door neighbours because we now clean for them, they told me about everything that has happened and, I am really sorry but no I can't help you with any new information!"

Jenson explained, "I guessed that Frank and Ella didn't tell you because they will be ashamed at what they have done to me!"

Margo replied, "I am going now before I get noticed and I lose my job!"

Jenson replied, "Okay thank you for letting us know, don't worry about your job because I will be back in charge again soon, I still can't get my head around how I was somehow trapped above my body watching everything below me while I laid there helplessly listening to everything being said!"

Margo left still talking as she walked, "Your welcome and yes it must have been frightening and strange for you to go through that odd experience that I hope that I will fingers crossed will never have to go through myself!"

Jenson followed Frank around everywhere being never far away from him ringing Ella, "Please tell Frank to meet me at the bank in an hour from now so that I can open a bank account for Violet!"

Ella replied, "Okay I will do."

Frank arrived at the bank just before Jenson, they walked in to the bank together with Jenson distracting him by pointing out what it looked like a crazy drunk lady stumbling about lifting her top and showing her breasts with the staff trying to cover her up with him unnoticeably slipping a gun into Franks pocket.

The banker lady behind the counter pointed at Frank and shouted, "Look he has got a gun everybody get down and hide!"

Frank just stood there oblivious looking around for the gun man.

Another banker lady shouted, "I will lock everything down."

A male security guard tasered Frank speaking, "Don't worry because he will not cause any more trouble today!"

Frank attempted to reply with hardly being able to speak, "It isn't me, oh where did that gun come from, it feels like something is crawling inside of my skin and I can hardly move."

The shutters banged shut all around them and the police arrived taking Frank away dragging him most of the way with him unable to walk lifting him into the police car with him stuttering his words speaking, "You will be in the cold slammer locked up in our police cell for a while in between being heavily questioned."

Chapter eleven

Slow dancing

Jenson rang Ella, "Can I come to see Violet while Frank is with the police?"

Ella answered, "Yes if you like but you can't stay long she is in the pool with our nanny having her swimming lesson at the moment."

Jenson replied, "I am on my way now please open the gate!"

They put the phone down.

Ella opened the gate and Jenson drove on to the driveway, he then walked inside, "It is lovely to see you Ella."

Ella put her arms around Jenson, "I really have missed you, I will put some slow beat music on and light some candles so that we can finish what we started about four years ago, I couldn't show my passionate emotions for you when Frank was here, Violet will be swimming for another half an hour!"

Jenson stroked her face gently with his hands moving downwards entering under her top, "I guess that you are telling me because you have missed getting up close with me please dance with me, I have wanted to finish this off for years it feels magical."

Ella's hands moved downwards towards his zip on his trousers, "I am enjoying slow dancing with you, I hope that it doesn't spoil it too much having Franks baby inside of me!"

Jenson put his hand onto her stomach, "I was in a comatose, but I am back now, I have missed so much, and I am just happy to be with you, it isn't great you having someone else's baby inside of you but it isn't the babies fault!"

Ella unzipped his trousers and released Jenson's penis with Jenson speaking, "That feels so nice, please sit in the bath and suck my penis like you used to!"

Ella replied, "I am already filling the bath, I love your warm and supple lips they feel so smooth as I kiss them!"

Jenson stripped Ella and Ella stripped Jenson with Jenson replying, "I have locked the door so that we are not distracted or disturbed, I love the bones of you."

Ella stepped into the bath and sucked his penis with joy in between speaking, "I don't feel like I am missing Frank, he was just conveniently available in the hours of need, it is you that I need, when ever I was with Frank I always had a picture of you in my head, I love everything about you, your personality, your looks, your scent, your soft Yorkshire accent and even your scars do it for me!"

Jenson helped Ella out of the bath with them walking in to the bedroom shutting the door behind them with Jenson speaking, "Please lay on your side and I will stick my dick into the back of you inside of your warm clit so that I don't hurt the baby!"

Ella replied smiling, "You may hopefully set me off into labour with your amazing sperm, I have got a joke what is the difference between tiger woods and Father Christmas?"

Jenson replied, "We will find out because here it comes and what is the answer?"

Ella replied, "That felt so good, and Father Christmas stops after three ho's."

Jenson replied, "I like that, I can hear light footsteps behind the door!"

Violet shouted, "Mum where are you?"

Ella replied, "I am just talking with Jenson we will be out in a minute!"

Jenson and Ella got dressed then walked out to Violet with Jenson speaking, "I have come to see you for a while did you enjoy your swimming lesson and I hope that the pool is heated for you?"

Violet replied, "Yes thank you it was fun, and yes the pool is heated, I am missing Frank, but I am glad that you are here with us!"

Jenson replied, "I am glad to be here too, I have got a lot of making up to do, I have got a joke what does a cloud wear under its raincoat?"

Violet looked at Jenson, "What is the answer?"

Jenson replied, "Thunder wear."

Violet answered, "You are silly, I have got a better joke why did the little boy take his pencil to bed?"

Jenson replied, "What is the answer?"

Violet replied, "To draw the curtains."

Jenson laughed, "You have got some cool jokes Violet!"

Chapter twelve

Papers found

They sat and watched a film called dream changing then Jenson mentioned, "Let's go for a drive around the block together in my refurbished Ferrari, but it will feel a little bit strange with us being properly together the last time that I drove it!"

Violet replied, "Yes let's go for a short drive."

They went for a drive with Ella speaking, "It is just like old times but with our lovely daughter Violet."

Jenson replied, "Yes it was cool going around my familiar neighbourhood thank you."

Violet replied, "That is nice being called lovely daddy because I am, I loved it too being with my proper parents together!"

Jenson spoke leaving, "I like it that you love yourself as much as I love you Violet, see you soon my little sunshine in my life."

Three days later Frank was released on bail with him hitching lift's off random people back home with him shouting as he walked up the driveway, "I shouldn't have even been locked up, but I am glad to get out of that place, I don't enjoy being in the company of the police."

Violet walked up to Frank announcing that Jenson had been to see her, "I loved seeing my dad it was fun!"

Frank looked angry, "I can't stop him seeing you both because he is Violet's dad but I don't like him coming unannounced with no appointment Ella, please don't let him in again without my permission first!"

Jenson sneaked through the open gate and entered the open front door and listened to Frank and everything going on.

Franks phone rang, he answered speaking to the person at the other side, "Yes now that I am finally back I will go and remove the paperwork in the office in a minute and put it back in the safe, I got it out so that you could look at it again now that Jenson is back!"

Frank cut the phone off.

Jenson followed Frank through the open office door crouching down hiding under the desk whispering to himself, "I hope that you don't catch me sneaking about in my house!"

Frank moved some paperwork from the desk to on top of the safe speaking to himself, "I will sort it out later."

Frank walked outside to the front driveway with Jenson following him, Ella drove up to Frank, "I am going to the hospital for a baby check up now please come with me, Violet and her nanny are in the pool safely swimming away."

Jenson was hiding behind a bush in the garden listening for them to leave whispering, "Please leave faster."

Ella and Frank drove off slowly.

Jenson climbed through the large open window, then went in to the office talking to himself, "Bingo, I have finally found the papers that I need you shouldn't have left them lying about for me to find on top of the safe if you didn't want me to have them, it feels like I have won the lottery having the extra evidence that I need!"

Jenson looked at the paperwork with half an hour passing by fast, "I am so glad that I have them because I can go to a solicitor now with the correct evidence that I needed to screw him over and massively ruin his life even more!"

Violet and her nanny walked outside of the office door with Jenson hiding under the desk with him muttering, "Please don't find me."

The office phone had three loud ring tones coming from it with the nanny going to answer the phone with it stopping as she got to it with her speaking, "We need to go to your friends birthday party now Violet, I will just lock up because your parents will be back soon."

Jenson tried to get out, "It is strange everything looking similar, and this is so frustrating because I cannot open the door, I may as well take a rest on my sofa and watch some television."

Half an hour passed by with Frank and Ella arriving back with Ella speaking loudly, "I am so glad that the baby is okay!"

Jenson spoke to himself, "I have just had a brain wave I think that the spare key may be under the painting in the lounge like it used to be!"

Ella announced, "I thought that I heard someone whispering but maybe not."

Jenson hid behind the sofa.

Frank and Ella walked in.

Jenson whispered to himself, "Yes, I have got the key but it is too late to get out maybe."

Ella spoke loudly, "That is unusual because the television is on in the lounge that has never happened before and I didn't think that they would have time to watch television because they were in the pool just before they left, maybe we had aliens dropping in for a short visit!"

Jenson sneaked out of the front door unnoticed whispering to himself, "That was good because I made it undetected!"

Frank walked into the office, "I thought that I heard someone earlier rustling about in my office, I really do need to get those papers back now before it is too late!"

Chapter thirteen

Eviction

Jenson drove straight to the local solicitor in Wakefield, "Can you please look through this paperwork and listen to this phone recording, you can keep it if you need to for a while to find out if they have made any mistakes on the paperwork to make it not legitimate!

The solicitor spoke, "The phone call says different, but it all looks legitimate, but on the bright side because the solicitor was not as professional as they think they are, I have just noticed that they have missed a crucial line of writing out that is needed to seal the deal properly, that has done you a real favour I must confess!"

Jenson replied, "That is amazingly untrue, can you sort this out with me to prove that everything is still mine?"

The solicitor replied, "Yes I can do that now for you!"

Jenson replied, "How do I get Frank out of my houses?"

The solicitor replied,"You need to get an eviction notice out against him so that he has got to leave and you need to show him this line on the paperwork to prove that he has messed up big time!"

Jenson replied, "Can I do that myself or do I need your help?"

The solicitor replied, "Fill this form in and submit it to the Leeds authorities with this paper work, they will then contact Frank saying that he needs to leave by a certain date, if he doesn't leave you can pay the bailiff's to get him out!"

Jenson drove back to Lucas's house then filled in and sent the paperwork off that was needed.

There was a knock at Lucas's door, Frank was stood at the door, "You have somehow got in my home and you have stolen my paperwork proof that I own everything that you owned and I need it back now or you will regret not giving me it!"

Jenson laughed replying, "The other day I went to the sports arena and it was very windy with the amount of fans causing a smelly wind, maybe some of them followed you and blew the paperwork out of the window, in other words you are not having it back, you have stolen everything from me and you will be back in the gutter where you belong soon because you badly slipped up by stealing everything that I own, I heard everything that you said while I was laying in the hospital bed feeling helpless."

Frank barged his way into the door, "Where have you hidden the paperwork tell me now?"

Lucas walked in to the room, "I heard you demanding your paperwork, you are not having it now get out I think that you have caused enough trouble, every time you look in the mirror you can see an asshole looking back at you because that is what you are!"

Frank replied, "Your daughter Violet is in danger if you don't cancel that eviction notice I will make your life hell."

Lucas opened the front door with Frank leaving muttering, "You want a big battle fight over who will have the best life I will win hands down one hundred percent because everything is still in my name."

Jenson replied, "I am glad that he has gone, I don't want him to hurt Violet, and we need to re kindle our love as a family!"

Lucas replied, "Frank will not hurt Violet because he has brought her up from a baby!"

Ella turned up at Lucas's home with Jenson opening the door, "Please listen, I only got with Frank because I thought that you weren't coming back but I have already given you a taste of me recently!"

Jenson replied, "I am glad that you are here, do you still love me Ella because I have always loved you?"

Ella replied, "How could I not love you we had mad passionate sexy love and built a cleaning business together before your accident that is still going strong thanks to us."

Jenson replied, "You need to keep an eye on Violet because Frank is threatening to hurt her!"

Ella replied, "I will go back home now to make sure that she is Okay."

Jenson replied, "I am glad that you are on my side, I will give you my new phone number that I have just got so that Frank can't contact me."

Ella left.

Half an hour ticked by.

Ella rang Jenson, "Frank has got fireworks that we were going to set off when our baby has arrived, he is in the lounge with a lighter threatening to light them!"

Chapter fourteen

Unborn

Jenson replied, "Oh my god Frank is trying to blow my house up I am on my way to you now!"

Ella replied, "Someone has just put a piece of paper on our front door, I guess that it is an eviction notice for Frank to vacate!"

Jenson arrived putting the phone down speaking, "I will call the police, the fire brigade and the mental health team because you are obviously psychotic Frank!"

Frank replied, "You will not stop me it is too late, we will all have nothing instead!"

Violet replied, "Daddy Frank please don't destroy our house and kill me, and my mummy, I really don't want to die."

Frank suddenly looked down at Violet crying, "You are right I will kill your unborn sister as well, so I will just leave while I can before they take me away, please give me some money so that I can run Jenson."

Jenson laughed, "I think that you have had enough off me, you are getting nothing else from me."

Ella replied, "I need that ambulance now because my waters have just broken and I can feel the baby leaving my body, I think that your special unique magic juices worked Jenson!"

Violet replied, "What magic juice is that please show me because I want some, and that is amazing my new sister is about to arrive with us!"

Ella replied, "It is just a joke between us Violet, don't worry about it, I used to work for an orange juice factory but I got sacked because I couldn't concentrate."

Violet replied, "Really mum."

Ella replied, "No it was a joke Violet."

Violet replied, "Oh yes I get it now orange juice is concentrated."

Ella replied, "I am sorry to burst your bubble Frank but you are about to be arrested say goodbye to your unborn daughter and Violet!"

Sirens were a short distance away.

Frank was sweating with panic, "All I can do now is run away or stay, either way I am going to be between a rock and a hard face to face the music in the end!"

Frank started to run out of the door with a police man grabbing hold of him, "Are you Frank?"

Frank didn't reply nodding up and down."

The police replied, "Has the cat got your tongue, is that a yes or a no?"

Frank replied, "Unfortunately yes I am Frank."

The police man replied, "I am arresting you for attempting to burn down

Jenson and Ella's house, the mental health team are here to assess you and by the looks of it you are not welcome here with an eviction notice against you, and you have attempted to try, and rob the Wakefield bank!"

The mental health lady spoke, "You need to come with us in our van, I think that you will be locked up for a long time!"

Jenson spoke over the phone, "At least we have got rid of Frank, I have missed enough time with you, I will come over and tidy up with you and live back in my house with you, I will meet you at the hospital!"

Ella replied, "Thank you for your support Jenson, at least you can hold my hands as I give birth, the nanny will look after Violet!"

Jenson replied, "See you soon."

Ella replied, "I have missed your cuddles and speaking with you."

Jenson arrived at the hospital, "I am happy to be with you, I will take on Franks baby like he did Violet, just one more push and the baby will be out, I am pleased to announce that I can see the babies head coming out!"

Ella replied, "I am just happy to be here with you, there should be someone changing all of the locks so that Frank can never enter inside of our house again, I am just thinking if a locksmith goes on strike does he refuse to picket?"

Jenson commented, "You are funny Ella."

Ella replied, "I do try, and I am pushing the baby out in a minute because I have got the feeling that I need to push."

Chapter fifteen

Stolen phone

Jenson's phone rang with Frank on the caller identification, "I don't know how you have got my number, or how you are even ringing me, but it is my turn to watch your baby being born to make up for me not seeing Violet being born!"

Frank replied, "I looked at your number on Ella's phone and wrote it down when she weren't looking before I left, I put the piece of paper with the number on it in my underpants to keep it safe and I have just got out of the van that we were in because the driver blacked out at the wheel, and we ended up hitting the car in front killing everyone but me, so a lady dragged me out and I ran off after I had stolen a phone from one of them."

Jenson replied, "Don't bother coming back here because the police will take you away again to a different mental health team and listen that crying is the sound of your baby being born that you will not see!"

The phone went dead.

Ella spoke, "Please phone the police and tell them what has happened!"

Jenson phoned the police informing them of all of the information, "I am confident that Frank will not come near to us."

Ella replied, "I hope not."

Jenson looked at the baby, "What are we calling this gorgeous little newborn girl?"

Ella replied, "I think that we should call her Sophia do you like that name?"

Jenson replied, "That is a nice name."

Ella's phone rang with Frank on the caller identification, "I will take Violet if you don't give me my baby girl!"

Frank put the phone down.

Jenson phoned the nanny and spoke with a low tone of voice, "Is Violet with you now and is Frank there with you?"

The nanny replied, "No just me and Violet are here has the baby been born yet?"

Jenson replied, "Yes we are calling her Sophia, you and Violet need to get out of there because Frank wants to take Violet, please go and hide in next doors house."

The nanny replied, "I will do that now."

They put the phone down.

The nanny walked next door with her being welcomed by them and stayed there watching with her peeping behind the curtain watching Frank through the upstairs bathroom window with her whispering, "Keep away from the window everybody so that Frank doesn't notice us."

Frank tried to enter through the gate of Ella and Jenson's house speaking, "I don't care what I have to go through I will definitely find you."

The nanny whispered, "It is scary listening through the open window, it is a good job that we left when we did, or we would be fighting against him to get away by now!"

Frank knocked on the neighbours door with no answer speaking through the letter box, "I know that you must be in there, you really can't hide from me!"

They ignored the door with Frank leaving.

Ella stayed in hospital for a rest.

Jenson drove in to his driveway then walked up to Frank speaking, "You have got no chance of finding Violet she is far away from here!"

Frank replied, "All of my troubles seemed far away not so long ago, I will find her, I bet that she is still in hospital and you have now stopped all of my bank cards, locked me out of my house, and stolen both of my children Violet and what is my new baby called?"

Jenson replied, "You mean my house, and she is called Sofia and that is all you will ever know about her now leave before I phone the police, and I am glad that you are having a taste of your own medicine that you gave to me, it isn't very nice is it being treated like dirt."

Chapter sixteen

Sophia

The nanny phoned the police whispering, "Please come now because we are in danger!"

Frank replied, "Where do I go now?"

Jenson replied, "In the gutter, I really don't care."

Frank replied acting innocent, "You are still my best friend, it was the best option for me back then please forgive me!"

Jenson laughed replying, "You wanted me dead when you stole my money from my bank and my business."

Frank lied saying, "I was saving everything for you until you got better please believe me!"

Jenson asked for it transferring back to his account, "Do you really think that I was born yesterday and what were you expecting me to live on fresh air?"

Frank replied, "It is invested and you will have it back at some point, I will go and get my new baby Sofia if I can't have Violet."

Jenson replied, "You will not find my beautiful family, and they are definitely not your family any more because they don't want you, I am convinced that you will be arrested before you find my beautiful family that mean the world to me, you will be the lonely one with no friends or family."

Frank left muttering to himself, "All I wanted was a nice life by taking over your life temporarily hoping that you appreciated what I was doing for you!"

Jenson followed Frank, "There is going to be an accident in a minute because I feel like ripping your head off at this moment in time!"

Frank looked scared in the face at Frank, "What kind of accident?"

Jenson stepped onto the sit on mower that went four miles an hour starting it up, "I have locked you in the back garden with no way out for you, you will have to run to stay alive because I have got a drone that will chase you as well to knock you over so that I can run you over and hopefully kill you, you should not be here and nobody will miss you."

Frank ran screaming, "I deserve it yes, I am not sure what is worse being run over by a mower or being locked up!"

Frank fell over a spade that the gardener was using earlier, "This situation is getting worse for me."

Jenson laughed, "I didn't even need to knock you over that is good, I will let you decide, oops I have just ran over your legs what a bloody mess that you have made on my lawn!"

Frank screamed in pain, "To make it worse I can hear sirens."

Jenson replied, "Good riddance, it was an accident with no proof, so they can't lock me up for you getting in the way of the mower."

Two police men arrived, "We don't need to put handcuffs on you because you can't walk, we will phone an ambulance to take you to the local hospital where you can get better, then you can be locked up for most of your life hopefully!"

Ella was walking out of the hospital with baby Sofia as Frank was wheeled in with a police man either side of him, "At least I have met my baby."

Ella tearfully replied, "Yes it is the last second that you will see her and you will never hold her in your arms to get that fresh baby smell or the father and daughter bond, Jenson will do that instead with him enjoying every step in her future life!"

Frank got wheeled away.

Jenson went to the solicitor that Frank had fraudulently used, "You will be out of business soon with what you have done because all of this information will be in the newspaper and on the television with it being breaking news for all to see in a matter of days from now."

Jenson built a case against Frank getting the police involved with a police lady speaking, "All of the papers are signed, so we can't help you sorry about that."

Jenson went to court and won his cleaning business, houses, money and cars back.

Ella put the houses up for sale with Ella speaking, "We will move to Spain in the Costa Del Sol where we can't be found by Frank and start a new warm, sun infused long-lasting life together selling up here building our new cleaning business together over there."

Jenson replied, "Let's go and wave goodbye to Frank and rub it in that he will be there until he dies."

Chapter seventeen

Private investigator

They walked past Frank at the other side of the glass with Violet and Sofia waving with Violet crying, "It was nice knowing you, I hope that your legs get better soon, bye because I have got my real dad now."

Ella smiled with no words as they walked away.

They drove back to their Leeds home packing up the last items for their move to Spain with Jenson speaking, "A new chapter of our lives can start now!"

Jenson's phone rang, "It is the court Frank has got ten years in prison."

Ella replied, "Good we need to cover our tracks to make sure that we can't be found."

Jenson replied, "We have sold everything that he knew about and started a new life here so Frank will hopefully never find us, I feel confident that we won't have a fight on our hands to stay together being a family."

Ten years later on the day that Frank was released, "I will track them down with a private investigator."

Frank suddenly got run over by a car as he was about to cross the road with him going unconscious.

An ambulance turned up putting him in the back, the ambulance staff put a breathing tube in to his throat to keep him alive.

Frank spoke, "What am I doing up here looking down at myself with my hands being like clouds, I think that I am having a taste of my own medicine."

Ella read a newspaper with Franks face on the front page, "Look Frank is in the same position as you were in Jenson, I think that is called getting what he deserves."

Jenson replied, "I hope that he is looking down at himself from above like I did with nobody visiting him."

Jenson phoned Margo, "Please tell all of your ex work colleagues to visit Frank to make him feel ashamed at what he has done!"

Margo replied, "Yes I will do."

Ella and Jenson made up in the bedroom with him stroking Ella to start with, "I love our new life Ella, I am glad that the kids are asleep, I can't stop kissing your body from head to foot!"

Ella groaned back, "I am really enjoying every minute with you, you touch me so softly."

"Your breasts are so amazing Ella I detect that you must have started to orgasm already, you are so sensitive to my fingers with you jumping around the bed, you are amazing!"

"I admit it, yes you are correct, please let me suck your dick Jenson to give you some great pleasure as well!"

"Ooh ahi that feels so good with you gripping it tight with your mouth Ella!"

"I am going to have put my penis inside of your clit Ella before I eject my warm sperm inside of your warm welcoming mouth with your tongue teasing me as well with you licking it while you suck!"

"Your penis is lovely and solid as usual inside of my dripping wet clit, I can feel that your cum must be close with you getting faster thrusting inside of me Jenson."

"Yes it is shooting out of me now, that was amazing, we need to do that more often Ella."

"I really enjoyed that as well Jenson."

They finally arranged to get married with Frank watching them marry over the internet rubbing his nose in it with him being full of jealousy.

A year went by with Frank coming out of his coma speaking, "I am going to do a view tube video appealing for anybody that can tell me where you are, they will enjoy a free meal from me now that I am better."

Frank got tipped off by strangers that they ran a cleaning business in the costa del sol, "That is where I am going then."

Ella and Jenson were oblivious to what he was up to with Frank turning up at their door unable to enter inside but attempted to jump over the fence unsuccessfully, then attempted to break the cameras with no success falling off a box banging his head causing an aneurism to his brain but finally died.

There was not a sole that turned up at his funeral with the funeral director singing a song that Ella had made up.

I was stupid to think that I could steal Jenson's life.

What a waste.
They are still living the dream but look where you ended up.
What a waste.
It is what you deserve.
What a waste.
You broke Ella and Jenson's trust.
What a waste.
They carried on living life with plenty of sex.

About the author

Anita Kirk is from Yorkshire in the United Kingdom, she writes many book genres with unlimited talent to write anything, she loves swimming, line dancing, holidays, music, films, writing, reading and spending time with friends and family.

In a Quarter of a second and the glowing

rings, Sexy Antics, Sexy
shenanigans, Christmas sparkles and
Fun dance book one have been
written so far with many more
available soon.

Remember that you can follow and contact
Anita Kirk with any questions or

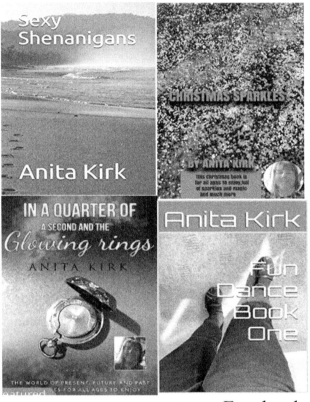

comments on Facebook, Twitter,
LinkedIn or you can email any
comments to anitajane1@outlook.com.
If you have enjoyed reading Anita Kirk's books
a good review would be appreciated and if
you could share Anita's books on your

social media, and with your family and friends she would really appreciate your help.
Thank you for your support reading this book. All of Anita Kirk's books are available on Amazon and some other online shops.

__A good review would mean a lot if you have enjoyed this book.__
__Thank you in advance for your review it is very much appreciated.__

Printed in Great Britain
by Amazon

14754582R00068